J.
COE OWL   COE, C

THE OWL'S of BLOSSOM
WOOD: THE
BIRTHDAY PARTY

Look out for more

The Owls of Blossom Wood

adventures!

The Owls of Blossom Wood

The Birthday Party

Catherine Coe

SCHOLASTIC

Echo Mountains

Badger Falls

Rushing River

Moon Chestnut

Oval of Oaks

The Great Hedge

First published in the UK in 2016 by Scholastic Children's Books

An imprint of Scholastic Ltd
Euston House, 24 Eversholt Street
London, NW1 1DB, UK
Registered office: Westfield Road, Southam, Warwickshire, CV47 0RA
SCHOLASTIC and associated logos are trademarks and/or registered
trademarks of Scholastic Inc.

ISBN 978 1407 15666 8

A CIP catalogue record for this book is available from the British Library

Printed and bound by CPI Group (UK) Ltd, Croydon, CR0 4YY
Papers used by Scholastic Children's Books are made from wood
grown in sustainable forests.

1 3 5 7 9 10 8 6 4 2

This is a work of fiction. Names, characters, places, incidents and
dialogues are products of the author's imagination or are used
fictitiously. Any resemblance to actual people, living or dead,
events or locales is entirely coincidental.

www.scholastic.co.uk

For Jessica Davies,
with lots of love xxx

With many thanks to the amazing team at the

Fritton Owl Sanctuary for your invaluable support —

and to your wonderful, inspirational owls.

Chapter 1

Rain, Rain, Go Away

"Done!" Eva put the final dollop of cake mixture into the last cupcake case with a grin.

Katie held back her long blonde hair and sniffed at the baking tray full of uncooked cakes. "Oh, I wish we could eat them now!"

Smiling, Alex shook her head at her

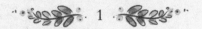

impatient friend, making her curly black
hair bounce about. "But they'll taste much
better when they're baked!"

Eva's green eyes lit up like gems.
"And then we can ice them – that's my
favourite part."

"Hi, girls," Eva's dad said to the three
best friends as he squelched into the
kitchen, his clothes and hair dripping.

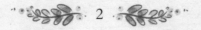

"It's horrible outside today."

Eva handed her dad a towel to wipe himself down. "Dad, can you put our cakes in the oven for us?"

Her dad nodded, spraying droplets of water over the kitchen tiles. "Of course. But don't forget about them this time!"

Eva's cheeks flushed red and Alex remembered why – last week Eva had made shortbread and gone over to Alex's while it was baking. Alex lived two doors down from Eva, and Katie's house was in between. Eva had only remembered the biscuits when the smell of burning floated across the gardens from two houses away. Eva loved making things, but she was also quite forgetful!

Katie held up her pink ballerina-shaped watch and pressed a few buttons. "I'll set a timer – then we definitely won't forget!"

"Good idea, Katie." Eva's dad slid the baking tray into the hot oven. "Right, I'm getting out of this wet cycling stuff."

As her dad padded up the stairs, Eva looked through the kitchen window. Raindrops poured down it like tadpoles in a race. "What should we do while we wait for the cakes?"

"I wish it would stop raining," Alex said softly. "I wanted to plant my daffodil bulbs today. But the ground is way too soggy!"

"I know," Katie sighed. "We haven't even been to look inside the tree trunk."

Alex grabbed Katie's arm, her brown eyes suddenly wide with worry. "But what if the feather's there? Shouldn't we check?"

Alex was talking about the magical feather that was sometimes left out for

them in the hollow tree trunk at the end of Katie's garden. It would whisk them off to an amazing and beautiful place – Blossom Wood – so they could help their animal friends who lived there.

Eva had already darted into the hallway. She came back waving a giant golf umbrella. "This will keep us dry!" As she pointed at the back door with the closed umbrella, she accidentally pressed a button on the handle. It shot open. Katie and Alex jumped back.

"Watch out!" Katie laughed, her blue eyes gleaming.

"Isn't it bad luck to open umbrellas indoors?" Alex pushed her feet into her ankle boots while Eva tried to pull the umbrella shut again.

"Oh, don't worry," said Katie, too excited to mind something like that. "Let's

just be quick!" She took the umbrella
from Eva so she could put her shoes
on too. Katie stepped out into the rain,
waiting for her best friends to join her.
The rain pattered on to the huge blue
canopy of the umbrella like a raindrop
orchestra.

The three girls huddled together as
they ran out of Eva's house and over to
Katie's next door. They pushed open the
gate and rushed down the path, past the
washing line, rabbit hutch and greenhouse
to the very bottom of the garden. When
they reached the tree trunk, Alex laid the
umbrella down carefully between the wild
flowers and dived into the hollow trunk.
Katie and Eva jumped in right behind her.

It took Alex's eyes a few seconds to
adjust to the gloom, but when she did,
she squealed. "It's here — the feather!" She

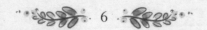

plucked it up with one hand and grabbed
Katie's hand with the other. Katie then
held hands with Eva, and they closed
their eyes shut tight. Alex's heart began to
beat as fast as a butterfly's wings, thinking
about what would happen next.

The spinning started gently, like the
slow twirl of a ballerina, but soon grew

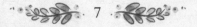

faster and faster, making the best friends feel as if they were on a super-fast roundabout, with wind rushing past their ears. None of the girls dared open their eyes as they were buffeted about, holding on to each other's hands and feeling their heads tingle and their toes fizz. Katie couldn't help beaming – she was so excited to get to Blossom Wood.

The spinning began to slow, and Alex's heart grew calmer. "Are we there yet?" she whispered.

"Not quite!" said Eva.

It was only when the spinning stopped completely and the wind had died to a whisper that the girls opened their eyes. Although here they wouldn't actually be *girls* any more – because every time they came to Blossom Wood, they magically transformed into owls!

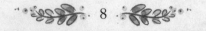

Eva's eyes flashed open. She was a pretty barn owl now, with a white heart-shaped face and light brown wings. "We're here!" she hooted as she balanced her talons on a high-up branch of the shiny Moon Chestnut tree. The woodlanders believed the Moon Chestnut was magical, because it had lived for a very long time – it was the tallest tree in the forest. On their first visit to Blossom Wood, the tree had been dying. But they'd solved the problem and now it looked healthy and strong.

Katie stretched her large snowy-white wings, speckled with black. She was an elegant snowy owl, the largest of the three friends. She blinked her orange eyes in the warm, bright sunshine. "Wow – the weather is so much nicer here than it is at home. It feels like summer!"

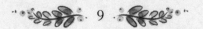

Alex shook her feathers out and flapped her brown wings. She was the smallest of the three – a little owl with a fluffy body and a tiny head that bobbed about a lot. "I feel so bad we didn't check the tree trunk until now," she said.

"Hopefully Bobby hasn't been waiting too long," said Katie, thinking about how she hated waiting for anything. She

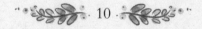

looked around at Blossom Wood, which seemed to sparkle like glitter under the sun's rays. Across the beautiful green treetops, Willow Lake glistened in the distance and the snow-capped Echo Mountains rose up over the horizon.

Eva glanced down the tree, searching for their badger friend. The trunk bent around in a crescent-moon shape, which gave the tree its name. "Maybe he gave up waiting? I can't see him anywhere!"

"Oh, owls, you're here!" came a voice. But it wasn't Bobby's. It was much too squeaky for that.

Alex spun around on one leg, and saw a grey squirrel bounding along a branch towards them. "Loulou!"

The squirrel skidded to a stop just above them and waved a paw. "It's so good to see you!"

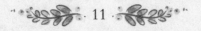 11

Katie waved a wing back. "You too, Loulou — but have you seen Bobby? We're wondering why he asked us here..."

Loulou put her paws to her cute, furry face. "Actually, it wasn't Bobby who called you here — it was me."

Alex felt her talons tremble with worry.

"What's happened? Is something wrong with Bobby?"

Loulou shook her tail frantically. "Oh no, nothing like that! I'm so sorry to worry you! Nothing's wrong at all. It's the opposite, really! You see, it's Bobby's birthday tomorrow, and we want to have a surprise party for him."

"What a lovely idea!" Eva twittered.

"We thought it would be," Loulou replied. "But we're having a few problems getting everything sorted. I hoped you might be able to help..."

Katie did a little hop of excitement on the chestnut tree branch. "Of course we will!"

Eva nodded. "We'd love to!"

But Alex didn't reply – not because she didn't want to help, but because she'd spotted something stripy on the ground far below them. "It's Bobby!" she whispered.

Loulou's pretty black eyes grew huge in alarm. "Oh no, he can't see you. It'll ruin the surprise – he'll wonder why you're here. Quick, owls, hide!"

Chapter 2
The Surprise

Loulou darted down the tree trunk, so fast she was almost a blur, while the three friends crept along the branch and tried their best to hide among the glossy leaves. It was easy for little Alex to keep out of sight, but trickier for Eva, and much harder for Katie. The snowy owl crossed her talons, hoping that Bobby didn't look up.

Loulou's and Bobby's voices rose
up from below. "Hi, Bobby!" Loulou
squeaked. "What are you up to? Isn't
it a lovely day? I thought you might
be relaxing by Badger Falls in such hot
weather!"

Alex noticed that despite the warm
sunshine, Bobby was wearing his scarf as
usual. Above it, she saw his black-and-

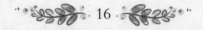

white head nod. "I was there a little earlier," he replied in his low, gravelly voice. "But I decided to go for a little stroll – you know, say hello to a few folk, see what everyone's doing."

"Oh, right, well, we're not up to much – not much at all. In fact, it's very quiet – very quiet indeed! Nothing to see around here!"

Katie groaned inwardly. Loulou was chattering even faster than normal as she tried to keep the surprise a secret – but would her panicking give it away?

"Ah, all righty then." He gave out a long, deep sigh, unlike his usual jolly self, and turned to leave. "I'll go on my way… Perhaps I'll look in on the creatures over at Willow Lake."

"No! Don't! Err, I mean … I … um … have a favour to ask." Loulou scampered

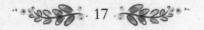

after Bobby. "Would you be able to collect some star fruit for me? You see, I need them for a cake, but they're too big for me to carry."

Bobby frowned. "But there's no star fruit around here – I'd have to cross the Great Hedge, out of Blossom Wood..."

"That's right – would you mind? It would be the most enormous help! Thank you so much!" Loulou didn't really give Bobby the chance to say no.

The badger's eyes brightened then. "A star-fruit cake, huh? May I ask what it's for, Loulou?"

"Oh, it's ... um ... a ... er, gift for the bees. They've ... um ... given me so much honey recently I wanted to make them something to say thank you!"

"I see." Bobby's eyes dulled again, and

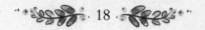

his mouth turned down at the corners.

Alex felt bad for Bobby. From the way his shoulders slumped, she could tell their kind friend was disappointed.

"I guess it might be good to stretch these old legs of mine," Bobby continued. "I'll be on my way to get the star fruit. Goodbye, Loulou." Bobby let one last sigh escape before plodding away towards the Great Hedge.

Oh dear, thought Eva. *He must have hoped the cake was meant for him!* Poor Bobby didn't have any idea the animals of Blossom Wood were planning a surprise.

"He thinks everyone's forgotten his birthday!" Katie whispered to her friends as they watched Bobby walk away below them. Eva and Alex nodded sadly. That was the problem with surprise birthdays. The birthday person – or animal – didn't know what excitement was in store for them!

When Bobby had disappeared out of sight, Eva, Alex and Katie leapt off the branch and flew down to Loulou. It felt amazing to be flying again, wings outstretched, feathers rustling, floating on the breeze. Katie, the most daring of the three friends, did a triple loop as she headed towards the ground, landing neatly next to Loulou like a gymnast. Alex wasn't quite so acrobatic, although she was much more confident at flying now than the first time they'd visited Blossom Wood. Her little body meant that she

could swoop between the branches, and she even did a little spin as she landed.

Eva zoomed down quickly, dived over a low branch and missed crashing into a bramble hedge by a feather's width. "So what can we help with?" she asked as she picked herself up.

Loulou opened her arms out wide. "Everything!" she squeaked. "It's not that the woodlanders don't want to do anything for Bobby's birthday – they're all really excited. But they're not very good at organizing themselves, and they won't listen to a silly little squirrel like me!"

"I'm sure that's not true!" tweeted Alex, putting a wing around Loulou's shoulder. "But we'd love to help anyway. We'll go and visit everyone right now, and make sure everything's on track for the party."

Katie clapped her huge white wings

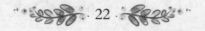

together. "I love parties! I'm so glad you asked us here, Loulou."

"At least Bobby's out of the way now," Loulou said, smiling. "I hope he isn't too annoyed about me asking him to run that errand, but I had to think of something quickly to get rid of him!"

Eva nodded. "It was a good idea to get him away for a while. It means we can sort everything out without worrying he'll come around the corner any minute. I thought he was going to spot us up in the Moon Chestnut tree just then!"

The three best friends began hopping along the ground and fluttering their wings, quickly rising up into the air. "We'll be back soon, Loulou," Katie called over her great white wing as she soared into the bright blue sky.

The squirrel grinned and gave them a

wave. "I'd better get on with the blueberry cake I'm making – this one IS for Bobby!"

"Let's go to Willow Lake first," Eva suggested as they flew over the treetops.

They passed the dark green trees of Pine Forest and the fruit-filled trees of Apple Orchard far beneath them. When they landed by a silvery willow tree at the side of the lake, they noticed everyone was rushing about madly.

They bumped into Jonny first – a friendly beaver they'd met last time they were here, when they'd helped find Flo, a baby deer who'd gone missing. "I'm making Bobby a maple cake for his surprise tomorrow!" Jonny told the owls proudly, before twitching his nose and rushing off.

Alex watched the creature scamper away through the grasses. "Loulou's making a cake too, isn't she? Although I

guess there are so many creatures in the wood that we'll need a lot."

"And you can never have too much birthday cake!" hooted Katie.

Eva pointed a wing towards the water,

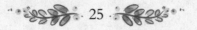

which was glistening like a mirror in the sunshine. "Let's go and see what the frogs are doing."

They skipped closer to the lake edge, where the water lapped at the grassy bank. Hundreds of toads and frogs hopped from lily pad to lily pad.

Katie cupped her wings to her beak to carry her voice across the lake. "What are you up to?" she called.

The jumpy creatures didn't stop, but cried together, mid-leap: "Making a cake for Bobby!"

Eva's beak drooped. "Oh dear. Is everyone making Bobby a cake? What about the other party things?"

A swarm of bees buzzed past just then. "Hey, Bella!" twittered Alex, recognizing one of the creatures.

The shy little bee stopped in the air, and turned. "Hello, Alex," she buzzed softly.

"Are you helping prepare for Bobby's party?" Alex asked.

Bella nodded her yellow-and-black-striped head. "We're making honey cupcakes − it's a bee speciality." Bella looked over her shoulder − the rest of her swarm were in the distance by now. "I've got to go − see you later!"

The three best friends looked at each

other in alarm. Everyone was making cakes! But what about the decorations and the music and the games?

"I'm starting to understand what Loulou meant about having trouble organizing everyone," hooted Katie. "Maybe there is such a thing as too much cake!"

"Look." Eva had spotted Flo and her mother, Sara, along with Flo's brothers and sisters, in a clearing away from the lake. "At least the deer don't look like they're baking anything!"

The friends fluttered over to the family. They were lining up planks of wood into triangular shapes.

"Hi, Sara, hi, Flo! What are you up to?" asked Eva.

Flo jumped up, her eyes bright. "We're building an ... an ... abstable course, for Bobby's birthday party!"

Sara smiled at her daughter. "You mean an *obstacle* course, Flo." She turned to the owls. "I hope Bobby likes it!"

Alex looked at Eva and Katie without replying. How could they tell the deer that an obstacle course might not be the best party game for an old badger like Bobby?

Chapter 3

Planning the Perfect Party

The three best friends were so busy for the rest of the day, they felt like their wings never stopped flapping. First they had to explain gently to Flo and Sara that the obstacle course might not be quite right. Luckily the animals quickly understood and the deer started using the wood to make tables and chairs for the party instead.

Next, Katie, Alex and Eva went to see Charles, the music teacher of Blossom Wood. The blackbird had tried to teach the owls how to sing once, when the wrens had lost their voices and couldn't sing their part in the Birdsong Concert. They'd quickly discovered Charles could be a rather grumpy chap, but they'd made friends with him eventually.

"Mr Blackbird?" Katie called, as the owls landed on the leafy ground beside his home in Apple Orchard.

"Who's that?" came a low, snooty voice.

Katie took a deep breath and carried on, reminding herself what Bobby had told them — that the blackbird's twit was a lot worse than his tweet. "We were wondering if you're doing anything for Bobby's birthday?"

The blackbird's orange beak poked out from behind the thick trunk of a Granny Smith tree. "Well, yes, of course! I've been collecting nice ripe apples all morning to make a birthday cake."

Alex couldn't help but bob her head with worry. Charles noticed, and frowned. "Why – what could be wrong with that?"

"I'm sure it'll be delicious, Mr Blackbird, but the problem is that *everyone* seems to be making Bobby a cake," Alex twittered gently. "And there are so many other things that need to be prepared for the party."

The glossy blackbird hopped closer to the three friends and peered at them. "I see." He paused. "That does sound rather tricky. But I'm sure I can use the apples for something else. How about I organize the music instead?"

Eva's heart-shaped face broke into a beam. "That would be fantastic, Mr Blackbird."

He nodded. "Leave it with me." Charles

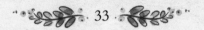

umbrella and daisy flower baskets, I bet they'd do a brilliant job!"

It was an excellent plan. Winnie and the rest of her wren family were delighted to help, and they quickly set to work. They began picking glossy leaves, pretty flowers and delicate grasses to make garlands and lanterns for Foxglove Glade, where Bobby's party would be held.

The owls thanked the birds and continued on their mission, flying around the wood and getting everyone organized. Soon, the dragonflies and fireflies were in charge of the lighting, and the rabbits were preparing drinks, making sure there would be an endless supply of blueberry cordial, for that was Bobby's favourite. By the time the sun began lowering in the royal-blue afternoon sky, it was just the party games that needed sorting.

Katie, Alex and Eva were swooping over the wood, wondering who to ask to help, when they heard squeaks coming from the Oval of Oaks below them.

The three best friends ducked their heads and tipped their wings one way, then another, floating gradually to the ground. With their excellent owl eyesight, they soon found out where the squeaks came from – it was two mice called Mo and May. When Eva, Alex and Katie had stayed overnight in the wood on an earlier visit, these sweet little creatures had brought them nettle milk to help them sleep.

"Hello, owls!" Mo squeaked. "We want to do something for Bobby's birthday, but we're not sure what…"

Katie landed with a bounce on the mossy ground beside the mice and grinned. "We have just the job. Party games!"

Mo and May twitched their ears and clapped their little pink paws. "Oh, yes — that sounds like great fun!"

May looked up in thought. "But what kinds of games? We mice like to play hide-and-seek — but I'm not sure that's such a good game for a big badger like Bobby..."

"You're right," said Eva. "But what games would be right for him?" Everyone fell silent, trying to think of ideas.

Alex was remembering her last birthday. First they'd gone to the local wildlife park and then she'd had a birthday tea at home. After they'd eaten the birthday cake, they'd played pin the tail on the donkey, but that might not be quite right here. "We could play pin the ... acorn on the oak tree?"

Katie jumped up. "Oooh, yes, that'd be perfect for Bobby! And how about musical ... toadstools?" Musical chairs was Katie's favourite party game – they could easily change it to work in Blossom Wood!

Eva opened her beak to speak. "What about pass the ... pine cone?" she suggested.

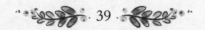

May squeaked. "Oh, yes, that's one of my favourites!"

The owls and the mice began working together to make the games. Eva flew off to Pine Forest to collect pine cones, while Katie went to find toadstools in every size imaginable to suit all the different-sized creatures of Blossom Wood. The mice gathered berries, seeds and other prizes to hide inside the pine cones, and Alex searched for fallen acorns, plucking them up with her talons to collect for the game.

By the time they'd finally finished preparing everything, the moon had risen high in the night sky. Eva, Alex and Katie flew back to the foot of the Moon Chestnut tree to tell Loulou that everything was on track.

The squirrel swished her tail about in happiness. "That's wonderful! As Bobby

would say, thank treetops you're here!"
She looked up at the round, bright moon.
"You will sleep over, won't you, and stay
for Bobby's birthday?"

The three friends smiled. Luckily, no
time passed at home while they were in
Blossom Wood, so they could stay without
their parents worrying. "Of course!" Katie

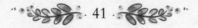

spun on the spot. "We wouldn't miss it for anything!"

Since they'd stayed in Blossom Wood before, Eva, Katie and Alex already had bedrooms ready for them – three pretty little hollows in one of the oak trees in the Oval of Oaks. They said goodnight to Loulou and flew to the tree, quickly nestling into the cosy, leaf-filled hollows.

"I can't wait to see the look on Bobby's face tomorrow when we surprise him with his party!" Katie called out from her bedroom. Usually, Katie hated going to sleep, but it had been such a busy day she couldn't keep her eyes open. "Goodnight," she hooted.

"Sleep tight," Alex replied.

"See you in the morning light!" Eva twittered.

When the three best friends woke early the next morning, the sun was only just tipping its pinky-orange head over the horizon.

But that didn't stop Alex. The little owl jumped out of her hollow on to a branch and shook her fluffy brown wings. "Katie, Eva, are you awake? Let's go and say happy birthday to Bobby!" Now that the day of his birthday had arrived, she didn't want Bobby to still be thinking the creatures of the wood had forgotten it. No one should be upset on their birthday!

Eva and Katie poked their heads out of the tree trunk, blinking their eyes in the sunshine. "Yes – let's go!"

They leapt from the oak tree and batted their wings to soar quickly into the air. Katie couldn't help grinning as they fluttered over Blossom Wood – no matter

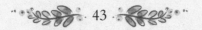

how much she flew, it always felt magical. Below them the wood spread out like the most beautiful carpet, and they could hear the first tweets of the birds' dawn chorus.

The three friends arrived at Bobby's sett, excitement bubbling like fizzy cola in their tummies.

"Bobby?" Katie hooted. There was no sign of life, not even a rustle, but maybe Bobby was still fast asleep.

Since Alex was the smallest of the three, she hopped easily inside the tunnel that led to Bobby's sett.

Outside, Katie and Eva heard their friend gasp. "He's not here!" Alex's little voice floated out from the burrow.

She ran back out of the tunnel just as a pigeon dived down from the sky. "Coo-coo!" it called. "Delivery!"

It swooped past, and without slowing at

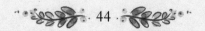

all, it dropped something beside the owls.

Katie looked down at the delivery – a piece of bark with writing engraved on it, attached to a net filled with strange-looking yellow fruit – then back up at the pigeon. It was now just a dark grey dot in the blue sky. "Was that a ... post pigeon?!"

The three friends giggled. "I've never

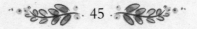

seen one of those before!" hooted Eva.

They gathered around the bark to read what it said — and the smiles suddenly fell from their faces.

Chapter 4
The Postcard

Dearest Blossom Woodlanders,

I'm sending you this postcard from the other side of the Great Hedge. I bumped into my second cousin George and he invited me to stay in his sett for a few days. I haven't had a little holiday in ages, and I must say, it's really rather nice. George is spoiling me with an endless supply of berries.

Warmest wishes,

Bobby (Badger)

PS The star fruit are for Loulou – please make sure she gets them safely.

PPS If there are no star fruit attached, I'm afraid the pigeon might have eaten them. He looked rather hungry.

"Oh no!" Alex put her head in her wings. "Bobby's going to miss his birthday party!"

"Maybe we could postpone the party? For when he's back?" Eva suggested.

Katie shook her snowy-white head. "But that won't be the same!"

"We should go and tell Loulou," said Alex. "Maybe she'll have an idea."

Her friends nodded in agreement. Katie plucked up the net in her talons, bulging with funny-shaped yellow star fruit, while Eva grabbed the postcard in her beak. They took off into the sky, to the growing sounds of beautiful birdsong, the sun now fully over the horizon.

How can we save Bobby's party? Alex worried as she fluttered along. Flying was always wonderful, but it didn't feel quite so magical when they had such bad news to deliver. At least it wasn't too far to Loulou's home in the Moon Chestnut tree.

The three best friends landed at the base of the tree, near a group of robins. The birds stood in a circle, practising "Happy Birthday", using different harmonies that made it sound even more fun than usual. No one could bear to tell the robins that there would be no need for the song today after all.

"Loulou!" Katie hooted, searching the bright green, glossy branches of the tree for the squirrel.

A bundle of fur suddenly shot down the trunk. "Hello, owls!" squeaked Loulou, her tail twitching so much that Alex thought it might drop off. "I'm so excited for Bobby's party today. I can't wait to see the look on his face!"

Katie sighed deeply, wondering how to

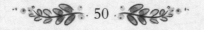

tell the squirrel their news.

Loulou's tail slowed to a stop. "What? Is something wrong?"

Eva set down the postcard at Loulou's feet. "I'm afraid so. Bobby's gone on holiday!"

Loulou read the letter, squeaking here

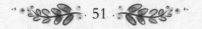

and there as she did so. "Oh, Bobby!" she squealed when she'd finished. "He can't miss his own birthday party! And he's such a kind badger to have collected the star fruit for me, even though he thought we'd forgotten his birthday."

"We were hoping you might have an idea of what we can do," said Alex.

The squirrel stared at the bark of the postcard. "Well, we could send a letter back and ask him to come home, but postal pigeons are not very reliable – who knows when another one will be along to collect the mail!"

Eva looked into the cloudless sky. She could see plenty of blackbirds, sparrows, starlings and wrens flying around – but absolutely no pigeons!

Shielding her eyes with a paw, Loulou glanced at the yellow sun. "But it's getting so hot, all the cakes will melt if he's not back soon!" The squirrel's squeak got even squeakier as she spoke. "And it's tradition to give the birthday animal the bumps when they wake up. To bump them into their birthday!"

Eva imagined Bobby being given the bumps. Would he really let the creatures of the wood do that? She wondered how many numbers they'd have to count to – Bobby was always saying he was older than he liked to admit!

"I'll go!" Katie's shout broke into Eva's daydream. "If we can't find a postal pigeon, and we need Bobby back quickly, I'll go and get him."

Alex swivelled her head to her friend. "Really? Not by yourself! We should all go together."

"But I'm much faster at flying." Katie felt her feathery cheeks flush as she realized what she'd said. She hadn't meant to brag. "Not that it matters usually, and you're much better at other things, Alex – but we don't have any time to waste!"

Eva put a wing on Alex's. "Katie's right.

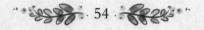

She'll be much quicker on her own." Eva turned to Katie. "If you're sure?"

Katie nodded her snowy-white head, feeling determined. She'd find Bobby and bring him back – and make sure his surprise birthday party went exactly as they'd planned!

Chapter 5
The Search for Bobby

Alex grabbed the postcard with her beak and passed it to Katie. "Take this. It might give you some clues to help find Bobby."

"Good luck!" Loulou called as Katie flapped her giant white wings and zoomed upwards into the air.

"Take care!" hooted Alex, bobbing her

head in concern. She wished they could
all go together! They'd never been over the
Great Hedge before. What if Katie got lost?

"See you soon!" tweeted Eva.

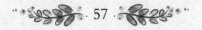

Katie waved a wing to her friends on the ground, then rose quickly over the treetops. Heading towards the Great Hedge, she passed the Oval of Oaks on her left and Pine Forest on her right. She couldn't see anything past the hedge, since it was almost as tall as the Moon Chestnut tree, and Katie wondered what she'd find behind it.

As the breeze ruffled her feathers, Katie's heart thumped with nerves. What if she couldn't find the badger? The whole of Blossom Wood was relying on her! Usually she'd spin and turn loop the loops as she flew, but there was no time for that today. She had to get Bobby back – fast!

She held her breath as she soared closer to the Great Hedge, and only let it out once she'd crossed it. Katie beamed at

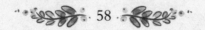

the sight. The other side was a blanket of trees and plants and flowers – greens and reds and purples and browns. The landscape whizzed by below her, blurring as she flew at top speed. It wasn't as beautiful as Blossom Wood – she couldn't see a glistening river or towering mountains – but it still looked pretty amazing from the air.

She spotted a fox, skipping along a grassy path below, and tipped her head to direct herself downwards. "Excuse me," she twittered politely as her talons landed in the soft, thick grass. "Have you seen a badger called Bobby? I need to find him urgently."

The brown fox shook her head and said, "Sorry – I don't know a Bobby!" and then scampered away.

Determined not to be put off, Katie looked around for someone else who

might be able to help. She noticed a purple-tipped butterfly fluttering around a patch of daisies. "Hello there, butterfly."

The delicate little thing turned at Katie's hoot, and flew right up to her face. "Oh, are you an owl? I've never seen one of you before. You're beautiful!"

Katie smiled. "Thank you. You're beautiful too! I was wondering … I don't suppose you've seen someone called Bobby about? He's a badger."

The butterfly's pretty wings turned down, as if he was frowning. "I've never heard of a Bobby — are you sure he lives around here?"

"Well, in actual fact he doesn't live here, he's on holiday…" Katie stopped. Of course no one knew where Bobby was, because they'd probably never met him before. But what was the name of Bobby's cousin? Katie took the piece of bark from her talon. "How about a badger called George?" she asked, feeling very glad Alex had suggested she take the postcard.

"Oh, yes, I know George! He lives in the badger burrows next to the poppy field — it's just a five-minute flight from here – though probably less for a big owl like you!" With one of his wings, the butterfly pointed behind him.

Katie smiled at the helpful insect. "Thank you SO much!" She took a few steps as a run-up, then flew into the air, and spotted the poppy field right away. A sea of orange poppies swayed like waves on their long green stems. Katie was surprised – she had always thought poppies were only red. She'd have to ask Alex. Her friend adored wildlife and knew tons about it. Maybe they were only orange here because the whole place was magical?

Five minutes later, Katie began descending down towards a large patch of brown soil beside the poppy field. As she got closer, the hope in her heart sank a little. The soil was dotted with holes –

clearly it wasn't just George who lived here. Going by the number of burrows, it must have been home to more than fifty badgers. But which one was his?

Katie fluttered to the ground, her talons kicking up the soil as she landed. "Bobby, George?" she called, waiting as patiently as she could. *Maybe I'll get lucky*, she thought. *Maybe Bobby and George will pop out right now...*

But no one – not even a flash of fur – appeared. Katie hopped closer to the nearest hole, but she didn't go in. It would be a squeeze to get down it, and anyway, she thought it'd be rude to just barge into a stranger's home.

She leant back on a nearby log and reread the postcard once, twice, three times, looking for clues. Bobby hadn't mentioned anything about where he was

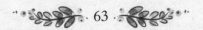

staying, other than with George. *Wait!* thought Katie. *He did say that George was feeding him lots of berries!*

She looked around at the ground again, hoping to spot a berry bush. But apart from the odd small patch of grass, there was nothing growing here. She swivelled her head once more … and that was when her brilliant owl eyesight spotted something. Was that a pile of pips just outside that hole over there?

While Katie was away, Eva and Alex tried to keep themselves busy. Eva made some extra-long daisy chains to hang around the flowers in Foxglove Glade. Alex collected together fallen leaves in the Oval of Oaks and used them to make Bobby a woven-leaf blanket for his birthday present. As the sun crawled higher in the sky, Loulou crossed all of the fingers on all of her paws, hoping Katie would return soon – with Bobby!

After Alex had wrapped Bobby's birthday present in lily-pad wrapping paper, she flew to Foxglove Glade to find Eva. The barn owl was hanging up her daisy-chain bunting. The foxgloves were

beautiful – every colour of the rainbow –
and in the bright sunshine they lit up like
candles. "Do you think Katie will be back
soon?" Alex asked Eva. "What if she's got
lost? Or hasn't been able to find Bobby?"

Eva draped the final daisy chain on
a lilac foxglove with her beak. "We just
have to hope harder than ever before.
Everyone's here ready – now we just need
the birthday badger!" Eva tried to sound
positive, but she was also worrying. *Where
are they?* she thought.

The two friends looked around the glade. Most of the woodlanders were there now, waiting for the party to begin, holding birthday cakes and presents, and carrying instruments to play in the birthday band that Charles had organized. But the celebrations couldn't start without Bobby!

Alex flew up, above the treetops, to look for any sign of Katie. Her little wings trembled when she spotted the elegant white shape of Katie in the very distance. "She's coming!" she called as she fluttered back down.

"Quick, everyone hide!" hooted Eva. "Katie's on her way back. I just hope Bobby's with her!"

The woodlanders stopped their chatter immediately and shuffled behind plants, flowers and trees to wait. The thick foxgloves hid most of the smaller animals,

while the bigger ones, such as the foxes and deer, used the tree trunks as cover. Alex and Eva hid in the branches of a sycamore tree.

Then they waited.

And waited.

And waited...

Chapter 6
A Birthday to Remember

The sun shone down, hotter and hotter. Alex noticed creatures jiggling around, getting restless — especially the little ones like Billy, a young, bouncy bunny. Alex turned to Eva with wide eyes. "Do you think Katie's found him?" she mouthed.

"Oh, I hope so!" Eva whispered nervously.

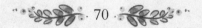

They looked up, waiting to spot Katie flying above them. But instead, Alex heard a rustling. At first she thought it was the movement of the fidgeting animals in the glade — but no, this sound came from behind them. As she swivelled her head to listen more carefully, a familiar gravelly voice rang out in the silence. It made Alex's heart leap.

"Where IS everyone, Katie? It's so very quiet. Are you sure everything is all right?"

"Oh yes, I think so," Katie replied in a high-pitched hoot. "Why don't you go into the glade — I think that's where Eva and Alex will be."

Eva hopped with happiness as the stripy-headed figure of Bobby the badger lumbered into the grassy glade. At the sight of all the pretty garlands and

lanterns, his jaw dropped open, and then everyone jumped out of their hiding places, into the glade, and yelled...

"SURPRISE!"

Bobby opened and closed his mouth, but nothing came out. He circled around slowly, and clapped his paws to his cheeks. Meanwhile, every single creature hooted and hollered and cheered. At one end of the glade where the grass rose in a sloping stage, Charles began conducting

the birthday band, made up of birds and insects and frogs playing pine cones.

They played the introduction to "Happy Birthday" and everyone started to sing. Alex and Eva flew down to join Katie, and they sang along too, even though they knew from experience that their owl singing voices weren't the most tuneful!

When the song finished, the birthday badger turned to Katie. He was grinning even harder than when they'd saved the Moon Chestnut tree. "Is this why you brought me back?" he asked.

Katie nodded. "I couldn't tell you the real reason. But we didn't want you to miss your own surprise party!"

"And I'm so glad I didn't! My holiday was very nice, but I don't mind admitting that I missed Blossom Wood, and all of

my friends. And there was silly old me thinking everyone had forgotten my birthday!"

Loulou ran up just then, carrying a giant blueberry cake in her paws. "Happy birthday!" she squeaked, passing the cake to the badger. He took a huge bite.

"Mmmmm, it's delicious!" Bobby said as crumbs dropped down to the ground. But the mess wasn't there for long – a group of little sparrows fluttered over and pecked the crumbs up!

Billy scampered towards Bobby and handed him a chestnut cup filled with blueberry cordial. "Happy birthday, Mr Badger!" Then the young rabbit turned to the owls. "When can we play musical toadstools? I've been practising!" He did a crazy little bottom-wiggling dance before plonking himself on the floor.

Alex smiled at the excited bunny. "Soon!" she told him.

Loulou took hold of Bobby's hand. "But first we must give you the birthday bumps!"

Suddenly Bobby was surrounded by animals, ready to lift him up into the air.

"Um … aren't I really rather too old for this?"

"Nonsense!" squealed Loulou. "You're never too old for the bumps!"

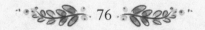

"One!" everyone shouted as Bobby was lifted up into the air.

He was quickly lowered, then lifted up again. "Two!"

"Three!"

"Four!"

And so the counting continued. By the time they'd got to twenty-five, Katie guessed that no one had any idea how old Bobby was! What's more, the dear old badger had started to look a bit green.

"I think that will do! Can you put me down?" Bobby called from mid-air, his face fixed in something between a grimace and a smile. "Please!"

The woodlanders lowered him to the ground and everyone clapped. *I don't think we'll ever find out Bobby's age!* thought Eva.

Bobby got to his paws and coughed for attention. "I was rather speechless earlier, but now I'd just like to say a few things. I thought you'd forgotten the birthday of an old badger like me – I was a bit sad about it, to be very honest… And so I am most overwhelmed and overjoyed that you were in fact planning such a wonderful surprise. You have made me feel very special, dear friends. Thank you, from the bottom of my happy heart to the tops of the trees."

The whole of Blossom Wood cheered once more, and Charles's band started up again. The many, many cakes were taken from the tables and passed around. And Bobby insisted on trying every single one of them!

Next, Bobby opened his presents, and oohed and aahed over them all – especially the blanket Alex had made for him. Then they played games, which lasted the whole afternoon. Bobby didn't stop smiling – even when Billy beat him at musical toadstools! And when the games were over, the band played hundreds of different woodland tunes. Katie, Eva and Alex had the best time

dancing with all the other creatures in the glade. Bobby even taught them how to tango!

As afternoon turned into evening, the fireflies and dragonflies lit up brightly over the party, making the glade look like it was filled with the prettiest fairy lights. With bedtime around the corner, the woodlanders began saying goodnight to Bobby and wishing him a very happy birthday for the final time.

Alex turned to her two best friends. "We should probably be getting home too."

Eva and Katie nodded. They hated leaving Blossom Wood, but now the party was coming to an end, they knew it was time to go.

Katie wrapped both of her huge wings around Bobby in a hug. "Happy birthday, Bobby!"

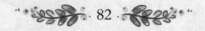

The badger smiled awkwardly – he wasn't really the hugging type – but he let Katie cuddle him anyway.

Once Katie let go, Bobby's smile stretched wider. "Thank you, owls, for everything you've done. It's been the most amazing birthday ever – one I'll never forget."

"And neither will we!" said Eva, giving Bobby a kiss on the cheek.

Alex fluttered up and shook the

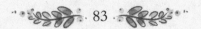

badger's paw. "Goodnight, Bobby. We'll be back as soon as you next need us in the wood!"

Katie, Alex and Eva took one last look at the beautiful Foxglove Glade before soaring up into the air towards the Moon Chestnut tree.

They came to rest on the branch they'd arrived on, held each other's wingtips and squeezed their eyes shut. Their talons started to fizz and the feathers trembled, and they felt themselves spinning round and round and round. As the air pushed past their ears, they could no longer hear Charles's band in the distance – just the whoosh of the wind as they spun and spun.

Eventually, they began to slow down, and when they finally stopped moving completely, they each opened their eyes. They were back inside the hollow tree trunk in Katie's garden, and girls once more!

As Katie blinked in the darkness of the trunk, her watch beeped loudly. She looked down at it and frowned – why was it beeping?

Behind her, Eva shrieked, "The cupcakes. I'd totally forgotten!"

"It's OK," said Alex as she emerged from the tree trunk first. She blinked at the pouring rain – so different from the weather they'd come from! "Time never passes at home while we're in Blossom Wood, remember? The cakes should be just about ready!" She grabbed the umbrella leaning against the trunk and hurriedly put it up to shelter them from the rain.

Eva jumped under the brolly. "Oh, yes. Thank treetops! Dad wouldn't be happy if I burnt them again."

Katie ducked under the umbrella too
and patted her full stomach. "As much
as I love cakes, I think we might have

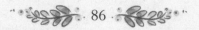

to give these ones away. After all those delicious birthday treats at the party, I don't think I can eat another thing!"

The three best friends linked arms and laughed. As they set off towards Eva's house, they all couldn't help but wonder when they'd get to have their next amazing adventure in Blossom Wood…

Did You Know?

🌸 It's true that poppies come in colours other than red — there are orange ones, yellow ones, pink, purple and even white ones. Have many different colours have you seen?

🌸 Pigeons really are used to send messages, because they have a great ability to find their way home. Before telephones and computers were invented, this happened a lot more, and they were even used in World War One to send messages between soldiers!

For more animal fun and games, check out the Owls of Blossom Wood website at:

theowlsofblossomwood.com